Published in the United States of America by Cherry Lake Publishing
Ann Arbor, Michigan
www.cherrylakepublishing.com

Reading Adviser: Marla Conn, MS, Ed., Literacy specialist, Read-Ability, Inc.
Book Designer: Melinda Millward

Photo Credits: © Elina-Lava/Shutterstock.com, back cover, 10; © Svetlana Turchenick/Shutterstock.com, cover, 5; © Luis Louro/Shutterstock.com, cover, 5, 19; © Kateryna Upit/Shutterstock.com, 6; © Andreus/Dreamstime.com, 9; © Nejron Photo/Shutterstock.com, 12; © duncan1890/istock, 15; © DM7/Shutterstock.com, 16; © GraphicsRF/Shutterstock.com, 19, 20; © vectortatu/Shutterstock.com, 20; © KI Petro/Shutterstock.com, 21; © Fernando Cortes/Shutterstock.com, 23; © draco77vector/Shutterstock.com, 24; © Edmensis/Shutterstock.com, 25; © pornpan chaiu-dom/Shutterstock.com, 25; © knape/istock, 27; © Fotokvadrat/Shutterstock.com, 29

Graphic Element Credits: © studiostoks/Shutterstock.com, back cover, multiple interior pages; © infostocker/Shutterstock.com, back cover, multiple interior pages; © mxbfilms/Shutterstock.com, front cover; © MF production/Shutterstock.com, front cover, multiple interior pages; © AldanNi/Shutterstock.com, front cover, multiple interior pages; © Andrii Symonenko/Shutterstock.com, front cover, multiple interior pages; © acidmit/Shutterstock.com, front cover, multiple interior pages; © manop/Shutterstock.com, multiple interior pages; © Lina Kalina/Shutterstock.com, multiple interior pages; © mejorana/Shutterstock.com, multiple interior pages; © NoraVector/Shutterstock.com, multiple interior pages; © Smirnov Viacheslav/Shutterstock.com, multiple interior pages; © Piotr Urakau/Shutterstock.com, multiple interior pages; © IMOGI graphics/Shutterstock.com, multiple interior pages; © jirawat phueksriphan/Shutterstock.com, multiple interior pages

Copyright © 2020 by Cherry Lake Publishing

All rights reserved. No part of this book may be reproduced or utilized in any form or by any means without written permission from the publisher.

45th Parallel Press is an imprint of Cherry Lake Publishing.

Library of Congress Cataloging-in-Publication Data

Names: Loh-Hagan, Virginia, author.
Title: Amazons vs. gladiators / by Virginia Loh-Hagan.
Description: [Ann Arbor : Cherry Lake Publishing, 2019] | Series: Battle royale: lethal warriors | Audience: Grades: 4 to 6 | Includes bibliographical references and index.
Identifiers: LCCN 2019003644 | ISBN 9781534147638 (hardcover) | ISBN 9781534150492 (pbk.) | ISBN 9781534149069 (pdf) | ISBN 9781534151925 (hosted ebook)
Subjects: LCSH: Amazons—Juvenile literature. | Gladiators—Juvenile literature. | Imaginary wars and battles—Juvenile literature.
Classification: LCC HQ1139 .L64 2019 | DDC 796.86–dc23
LC record available at https://lccn.loc.gov/2019003644

Printed in the United States of America
Corporate Graphics

About the Author

Dr. Virginia Loh-Hagan is an author, university professor, former classroom teacher, and curriculum designer. She wrote a 45th Parallel Press book about girl warriors. She lives in San Diego with her very tall husband and very naughty dogs. To learn more about her, visit www.virginialoh.com.

Table of Contents

Introduction 4
Amazons 6
Gladiators 12
Choose Your Battleground 18
Fight On! 22
And the Victor Is 28

Consider This! 32
Learn More! 32
Glossary 32
Index 32

Introduction

Imagine a battle between Amazons and gladiators. Who would win? Who would lose?

Enter the world of *Battle Royale: Lethal* **Warriors**! Warriors are fighters. This is a fight to the death! The last team standing is the **victor**! Victors are winners. They get to live.

Opponents are fighters who compete against each other. They challenge each other. They fight with everything they've got. They use weapons. They use their special skills. They use their powers.

They're not fighting for prizes. They're not fighting for honor. They're not fighting for their countries. They're fighting for their lives. Victory is their only option.

Let the games begin!

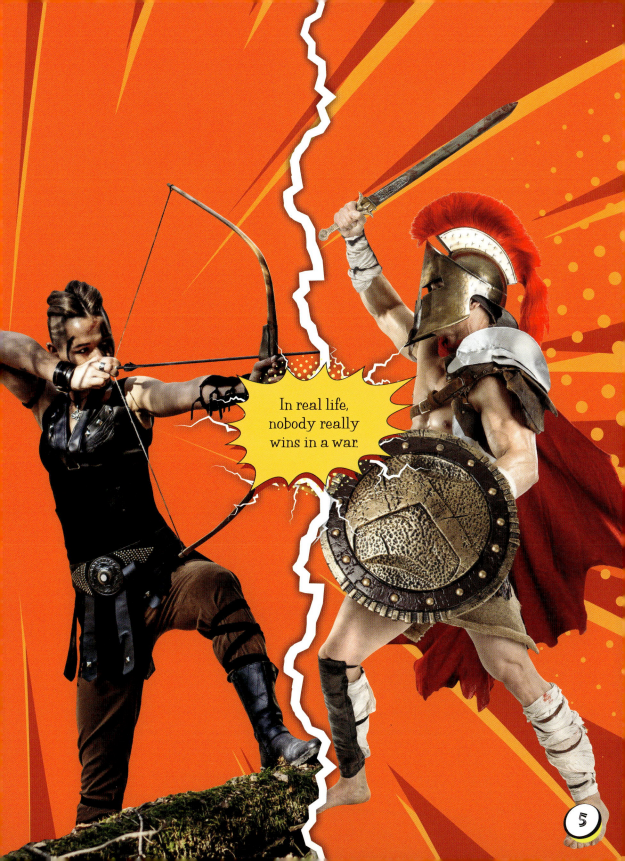

AMAZONS

Amazon is not a Greek word. It might be from an ancient Iranian word that means "warrior."

Amazons were a **tribe** of tall women warriors. Tribes are groups. Amazons were part of ancient Greek myths. But they may have been real. Scientists have connected Amazons to Scythians. Scythians were **nomads**. Nomads move from place to place. Amazons lived around northern Turkey. They lived in the **steppes** of central Asia. Steppes are dry, grassy plains.

Amazons were a girls-only club. There were no males in their group. Males were sent to other tribes. Females were sent to the Amazons. This was a common thing to do. Nomads sent children to other tribes. This process was called **fosterage**. It helped build good relations. It kept peace between tribes.

Amazons were born for war. They were wild. They were brutal. They prepared for battle. They started training at a young age. They never ran from danger. They never begged for mercy. Some stories say they couldn't marry until they killed a man in battle.

They were expert **archers**. Archers shoot bows and arrows. Amazons had a special bow. Their bows were small and powerful. Amazons threw spears. They used swords and daggers. They used battle-axes and shields.

Amazons tamed animals. They hunted with eagles.

They were strong land fighters. But they were better on their horses. They were expert riders. They spent a lot of time on their horses. Their legs were bowed from so much riding. They practice **mounted** archery. Mounted means on a horse. Amazons shot their arrows on horseback. This was a great skill.

Ancient Greeks believed Amazons invented pants. People who ride horses need pants. They need to cover their legs. Amazons wore pants. They also wore short dresses with belts. They wore jackets. They wore pointed hats with earflaps. They wore leopard and lion skins.

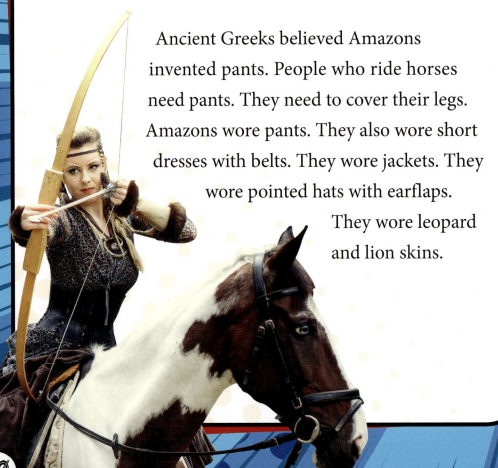

FUN FACTS ABOUT AMAZONS

- Amazon-like women had tattoos. Scientists were studying ancient Scythian burial sites. They found tattoo kits. They found frozen bodies of several tattooed women. An example is the Siberian Ice Maiden. Her mummy was found in 1993. She had tattoos of a deer on her shoulder. She had deer tattoos on her wrist and thumb.

- An Amazonomachy was an Amazon battle. There were several Amazonomachies between the Amazons and ancient Greeks. These battles represented civilization. Amazons were savage. Greeks were civilized. Amazonomachies were seen as an act of feminism. Feminism is the belief that women should have equal rights.

- Hippolyta was an Amazonian queen. Her name means "horse." Her father was Ares. Ares was the god of war. He gave Hippolyta a magical girdle. A girdle is a belt. It's worn around the waist. Hippolyta's girdle was a symbol of her power. It also gave her magical powers.

GLADIATORS

Roman nobles used gladiator fights to gain the love of the people. They promoted themselves.

Gladiators were trained fighters. They fought against other gladiators. They fought against wild animals. They fought in **arenas**. Arenas are areas for public events. Gladiators fought to entertain people. They fought to the death. These fights occurred in ancient Rome. They were called games. Many people watched gladiators fight.

Gladiator fights may have started as **funerals**. Funerals are events that honor people's deaths. Rich nobles hosted gladiator fights. They honored their dead with blood. They thought human blood cleaned dead people's souls. These fights became popular. They became bloody sporting events. They took place for about 500 to 700 years.

Most gladiators were **slaves**. Slaves are people who are owned by other people. Slaves had no choice. They were forced to be gladiators. They fought to make money for their masters. Some fought to buy their freedom.

Some gladiators were prisoners of war. Some were criminals. Some were free men. These men liked the thrill of the fight. They liked risking their lives. They wanted fame and glory.

There were gladiator schools. Gladiators learned to fight. They were taught to hurt, not kill. This was to keep games going. Gladiators turned pain into a show. They learned to fight given challenges. For example, they fought with one hand tied to their back.

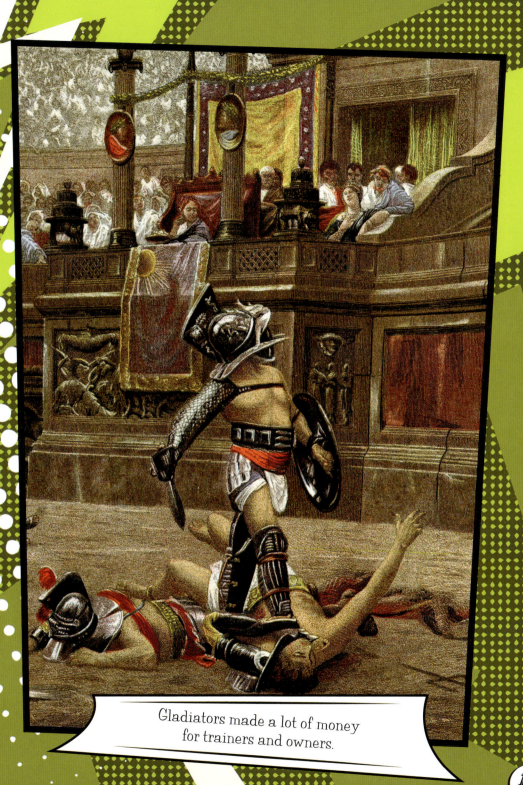

Gladiators made a lot of money for trainers and owners.

There were different types of gladiators. Some fought in pairs. Some fought alone. Some fought on horses. Some fought in **chariots**. Chariots are wheeled carts pulled by animals.

Gladiators wore **armor**. Armor covers and protects bodies. Gladiators knew how to use all kinds of weapons. They used swords and shields. They used nets and spears. They used metal gloves and ropes.

They had an honor code. They had to fight well. Or they had to die well. They couldn't cry out. They couldn't beg for their lives. Those who refused to fight were hit with whips or hot metal bars. They had a 1 in 10 chance of being killed. They didn't live long.

FUN FACTS ABOUT GLADIATORS

- Not all gladiator fights were fights to the death. Most fights had strict rules. They were like boxing. They matched up gladiators of the same size. They had referees. The referees stopped the fights when people were really hurt.

- Gladiators rarely fought against animals. There were special fighters who fought against wild beasts. But animal hunts were hosted in Roman arenas. The Colosseum is a famous arena. It's in Rome. On its opening day, over 9,000 animals were killed.

- There may have been female gladiators. A female gladiator is called a gladiatrix.

- Gladiators formed unions. Unions are worker groups. Gladiators promised to bury each other. They promised to take care of dead gladiators' families.

- Gladiators were like rock stars. Women dipped their jewelry in gladiator blood. They mixed gladiator sweat into their face creams.

CHOOSE YOUR BATTLEGROUND

Amazons and gladiators are fierce. They have similar fighting skills. Both groups have been treated unfairly. They didn't have the same rights as free people. Amazons are women. Gladiators are mostly slaves. Amazons and gladiators are well-matched. This would be a good fight. So, choose your battleground carefully!

Battleground #1: Sea

- Neither group can sail.

- There's a story about Amazons. Ancient Greeks kidnapped them. They jailed them in ships. Amazons escaped. They killed all the Greeks. They waited to land on an island. They raided nearby towns. They stole horses. They got back home.

- Sometimes, the gladiators' arena was filled with water. This was to put on a sea battle show.

Some gladiators were branded or tattooed.

Battleground #2: Land

- Amazons and gladiators are both good land fighters. They can fight on solid ground.

- Both groups can fight while moving. Both can fight while on horses. Gladiators can also fight on chariots.

- Gladiators are used to fighting in a small area. Amazons can fight in a larger area.

Battleground #3: Mountains

- Amazons and gladiators know how to fight on flat lands. They'd have a hard time climbing mountains. They'd have a hard time getting their gear up mountains. Amazons couldn't bring their horses. Gladiators couldn't bring all their weapons. Their weapons are heavy.

- Both groups are from warm areas. They'd have trouble fighting in cold areas. Mountains tend to be cold.

ARMED AND DANGEROUS: WEAPONS

Amazons: Amazons were famous for using shields. Their favorite was a pelta. Pelta shields were small. They were covered with sheep or goat skin. They were made from wood sticks woven together. They were shaped like crescents. Crescents are curved. They're broad in the center. They turn into points at the ends. Amazons were able to get a good attack angle. They could turn, lift, or duck. They could rest their spears on the curved end.

Gladiators: Gladiators used the gladius sword. This sword was used by Roman foot soldiers. It was made from iron. It was a straight sword. It was designed to be short, at 24 inches (61 centimeters) long. It was broad. It had 2 sharp edges. This was for cutting and chopping. The sword also narrowed down to a point. This was good for stabbing and thrusting. The handle had a solid grip. It had ridges for fingers. It gave gladiators good balance to slash with great force.

FIGHT ON!

The battle begins! Amazons and gladiators rush out. Amazons are on their horses. Some gladiators come out on horses. Some come out on chariots. Some come running out on their feet.

Move 1:

Amazons stay on their horses. They take out their bows and arrows. Their swords and spears are on their belts. One group circles around the gladiators on foot.

Ancient Romans also hosted chariot races.

Move 2:

Gladiators swing their weapons. They all have different weapons. They brought a cart full of weapons. They need to run back and forth to get their weapons.

Move 3:

Another group of Amazons circles the gladiators on higher ground. They all pull back on their bows. They aim. They shoot fast. The inner circle targets the gladiators inside the circle. The outer circle targets the gladiators on horses and chariots.

Women fought in Mongol and Hun armies. These women were similar to Amazons.

LIFE SOURCE: FOOD FOR BATTLE

Amazons: A popular food for Amazons was koumiss. Koumiss is fermented mare's milk. Mare is a female horse. Fermenting is a process. It's when food is pickled or aged. Mare's milk has more sugars than other milks. This means koumiss has a little alcohol. Mare's milk was put in a leather bag. Amazons rode with the bag. The riding mixed the milk. Koumiss is lighter than cow's milk. It's a little sour.

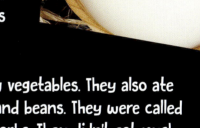

Gladiators: Gladiators ate mostly vegetables. They also ate grains. They ate a lot of barley and beans. They were called "barley men." They ate a lot of carbs. They didn't eat much dairy. They didn't eat much meat. Meat was expensive. It was hard to keep fresh. Gladiators drank a special drink. The drink was made from plant ashes. It was healthy. It helped them heal. It gave them energy. It made their bones strong.

Move 4:

Gladiators hold up their shields. They protect themselves from the Amazons' arrows. With their other hands, they thrust with their swords. They aim for knees. They aim for horses. They pull Amazons off horses.

Move 5:

Amazons team up. They fight back-to-back. They attack from all sides. They slash and cut with shields and swords. They move quickly. They move together.

Move 6:

Gladiators attack back. They move their shields aside. They stab. They bring shields back. They keep doing this. They aim for stomachs. They cut off arms. They cut off legs.

Amazons raided towns together.

AND THE VICTOR IS . . .

What are their next moves?
Who do you think would win?

Amazons could win if:

- They tire out the gladiators. Gladiators are used to fighting in short matches. They're not used to fighting in long battles. But they're used to getting hurt. They can take a lot of pain.
- They stay united. They have more practice fighting as a team. Gladiators are used to fighting for themselves.

Gladiators could win if:

- They get rid of horses. Some gladiators can fight on horses. But all Amazons are good fighters on horses. They're also better horse riders.
- They use different weapons. Amazons don't use as many weapons as gladiators.

Both Amazons and gladiators were trained to fight until the death.

Amazons: Top Champion

Penthesilea was a queen of the Amazons. Her mother was Otrera. Otrera was an Amazon. Her father was Ares. Ares was the Greek god of war. Penthesilea was the best warrior. She was brave. She knew how to use weapons. She's believed to have invented the battle-axe. She and her sister were hunting deer. She accidentally killed her sister. She killed her with a spear. She felt really bad. She wanted to die. The only honorable death was to die in war. So, Penthesilea led an army of Amazons. She fought in the Trojan War. She fought for Troy. Paris was a Trojan prince. He kidnapped Helen of Sparta. Helen's husband led an army to get her back. This was the reason for the Trojan War. There are different stories about how Penthesilea died. In one story, she fought against the Greeks. She killed Achilles. Achilles was a Greek hero. A Greek god brought him back to life. Achilles killed Penthesilea.

Gladiators: Top Champion

Spartacus was born in Thrace. Today, Thrace is Bulgaria, Greece, and Turkey. Spartacus was in the Roman army. He was sold as a slave. He trained at a gladiator school. He met other slaves. He became their leader. He led them in an escape. Spartacus continued to lead the slaves. He fought against Roman rule. He fought in the Gladiators' War. He freed other slaves. He convinced them to join his fight. His army had about 100,000 men. They did surprise attacks. Spartacus defeated many Roman soldiers. He fought them in France. He fought them in Italy. He was finally defeated. He was surrounded. He was killed in battle. This happened in 71 BCE. His body was never found. Spartacus became a hero. He's a symbol for people fighting for freedom.

Consider This!

THINK ABOUT IT!

- How are Amazons and gladiators alike? How are they different? Are they more alike or different? Why do you think so?
- If Amazons and gladiators lived at the same time, do you think they would've fought each other? If they did, who would've won? Why do you think so?
- Wonder Woman is a superhero character. She is based on the Amazons. How so? How does Wonder Woman's story diverge from the Amazon story? Diverge means to separate.
- Which superhero is most like a gladiator? In what ways? Why do you think so?
- Learn more about female gladiators. Why weren't there more females? Do some research. Find out.

LEARN MORE!

- Clayton, Sally Pomme, and Sophie Herxheimer (illust.). *Amazons! Women Warriors of the World.* London: Lincoln Children's Books, 2009.
- Lee, Adrienne. *Gladiators.* North Mankato, MN: Capstone Press, 2014.
- Malam, John, and David Antram (illust.). *You Wouldn't Want to Be a Roman Gladiator!: Gory Things You'd Rather Not Know.* New York, NY: Franklin Watts, 2013.
- Napoli, Donna Jo, and Christina Balit (illust.). *Treasury of Greek Mythology: Classic Stories of Gods, Goddesses, Heroes, & Monsters.* Washington, DC: National Geographic Society, 2011.

GLOSSARY

archers (AHR-churz) people who shoot bows and arrows
arenas (uh-REE-nuhz) large stadiums for public events that have a stage for performers and seats for spectators
armor (AHR-mur) body covering used for protection
chariots (CHAR-ee-uhts) carts with two wheels that are pulled by animals
fosterage (FAWS-tur-ij) a system in which children are sent to other families to raise in order to build alliances and create peace
funerals (FYOO-nur-uhlz) events or ceremonies that honor people's deaths
mounted (MOUNT-id) being on top of a horse or a moving vehicle
nomads (NOH-madz) people who move from one place to another
opponents (uh-POH-nuhnts) groups who compete against each other
slaves (SLAYVZ) people who are owned by other people and forced to do their bidding
steppes (STEPS) dry, grassy plains
tribe (TRIBE) a group or community
victor (VIK-tur) the winner
warriors (WOR-ee-urz) fighters

INDEX

Amazons, 30
    battlegrounds, 18–20
    battles, 22–27
    fun facts about, 11
    how they win, 28
    training, 8
    weapons, 8, 21, 23, 24, 26
    what they wore, 10
    who they were, 6–11

battlegrounds, 18–20
battles, 22–27

food, 25

gladiators, 31
    battlegrounds, 18–20
    battles, 22–27
    fun facts about, 17
    how they fought, 13, 14, 16
    how they win, 29
    weapons, 21, 24, 26
    what they wore, 16
    who they were, 12–17

opponents, 4

Penthesilea, 30

Spartacus, 31

victors, 4

weapons, 8, 10, 21, 24, 26
women, 7, 17, 18, 24